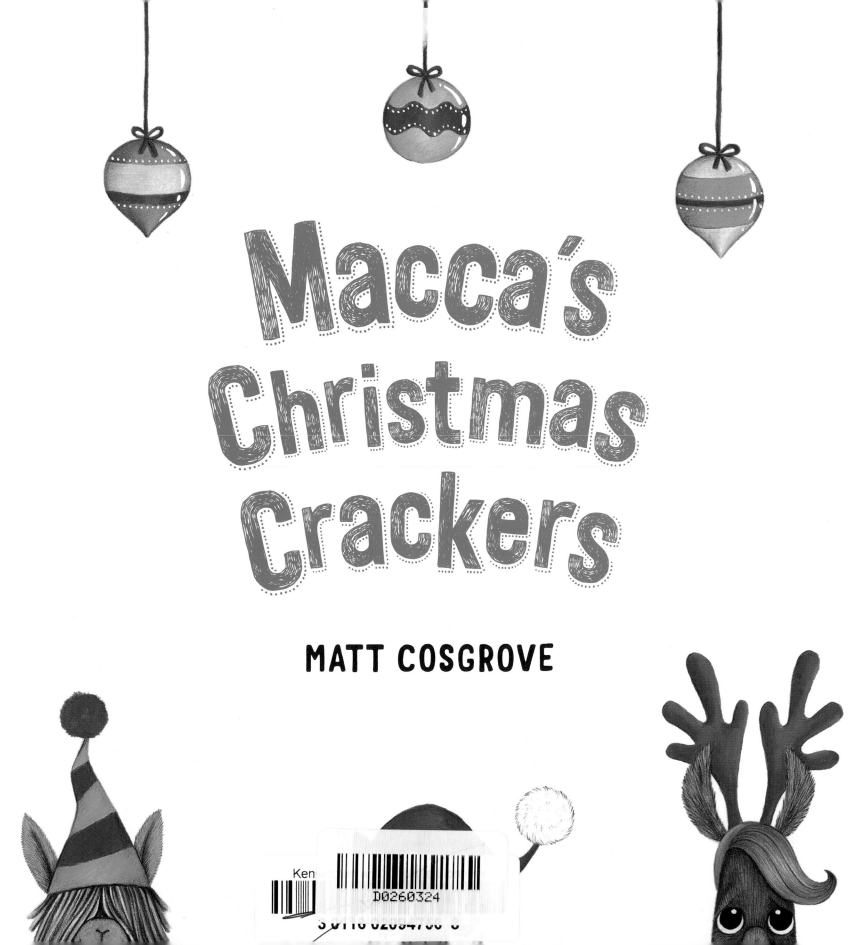

Macca's Christmas Crackers

MATT COSGROVE

For the best presents I ever received,
the Lion and the Hunter — love M.C.

First published in 2018 by Koala Books
An imprint of Scholastic Australia Pty Limited

First published in the UK in 2019 by Scholastic Children's Books
Euston House, 24 Eversholt Street
London, NW1 1DB
A division of Scholastic Ltd
www.scholastic.co.uk

London – New York – Toronto – Sydney – Auckland
Mexico City – New Delhi – Hong Kong

ISBN 978 1407 19777 7

Typeset in Mr Dodo featuring Festivo LC.

This guy is called **Macca.**

He's an alpaca!

He loves to **canter...**

And dress up like . . .

SANTA!

'Coz **Christmas** is here! The **BEST** time of the year!

Macca often confessed
He was Christmas

OBSESSED!

He **jingled** bells
and sang **NOELS!**

He decked the halls,

And floors,

AND walls!

Stockings were strung

MaCCA

AL

HARMER

PAT

NAT

MATT

BILL

JILL

WILL

FLO

JOE

MO

and wreaths were hung.

Tinsel was **tangled**
and baubles were **dangled.**

When it came to the tree

Not an inch was left free.

He scaled new heights with Christmas lights.

'Let it glow...'

But what Macca **loved best**
Of the whole Christmas-fest,
Was his reason for living—
the spirit of giving!

Oh goodness, oh my! There was **so much** to buy!

A **jetski** for Al, his daredevil pal.

Some **dumbbells** for Harmer,

That muscle-mad llama.

For Maxine and Jax, those sax playing yaks,
who loved to be cool—

an **inflatable pool!**

Alas for our hero,
His savings were . . .

zero!

Macca was **fraught!**
There were gifts
to be bought!

'I need presents
fast!'
(He'd left shopping 'til last.)

Al looked at that frown,
And calmed Macca down.

'You don't need to spend anything on a friend!'

'You're a real angel, Al,'
Macca smiled at his pal.

'Let's **make** what we can!'

So their workshop began.

And those clever alpacas
made their own

CHRISTMAS CRACKERS!

After Christmas dinner, everyone was a **winner!**
Beaming proudly, little Macca gave each friend a **cracker.**

'On the count of three, gang,'

And the **crackers** went 1, 2, 3...

'It's the **best CHRISTMAS** yet!'
Macca sheepishly shrugged,
and then they all . . .

...hugged!

(The best things, you see, are quite often free!)